Book design by: Dynagrafik Design Studios Ltd.

Audiobook produced by: HillelKAPS Productions (www.HillelKaps.com)
Audiobook recorded @ Uptop Studios (Monsey, NY)
Engineered and Narrated by: Hillel Kapnick

Additional Voices:
Shalom Frenkel
Tova Ganz
Gila Kapnick
Ahuva Shira Kapnick
Yehuda Kapnick
Aharon Eliezer Kapnick

Singing voices are male only.

Distributed by:
Israel Bookshop Publications
501 Prospect Street
Lakewood, NJ 08701

Tel: (732) 901-3009
Fax: (732) 901-4012
www.israelbookshoppublications.com
info@israelbookshoppublications.com

Printed in Bulgaria

Distributed in Israel by:
Tfutza Publications
P.O.B. 50036
Beitar Illit 90500
972-2-650-9400

Distributed in Europe by:
Lehmanns
Unit E Viking Industrial Park
Rolling Mill Road,
Jarrow, Tyne & Wear NE32 3DP
44-191-430-0333

Distributed in Australia by:
Gold's Book and Gift Company
3-13 William Street
Balaclava 3183
613-9527-8775

Distributed in South Africa by:
Kollel Bookshop
Northfield Centre
17 Northfield Avenue
Glenhazel 2192
27-11-440-6679

Middos Malka
Shalom in Our Homes

By Esther Ornstein

Illustrations by Racheli David

Audio book by Hillel Kapnick

Shlomo, Freida, and Leah were so excited. Today, lots of their cousins were coming over for a barbecue get-together. Even baby Eli was smiling in his highchair! Everyone was getting ready to set up the backyard.

Mr. Yetzer Horah was scooting around on his electric scooter, wearing a large, floppy sunhat and sunglasses. What a beautiful day to make some trouble! Mr. Yetzer Horah had some good ideas, and a big smile spread over his face.

4

The backyard looked amazing! There was a ball-pit set up, and a jumpy house, a trampoline, and a crafts table. The swing set was shining in the bright sun. So many fun activities to do together with the cousins! The speakers were all set up near the grill, and Abba put on some music for the kids to listen to until everyone arrived.

Mr. Yetzer Horah stopped his scooter and listened.
Hmm...he heard music coming from somewhere nearby.
As he came closer, he decided to stick around and see
if he could find someone he could convince to make
some mistakes.

6

"Leah," called Mommy, "would you please take these cups to the table outside? Freida, please take these plates outside, and Shlomo, would you take this pitcher of lemonade to the table?"

"Sure, Mommy," answered Leah and Freida. Leah came to get the cups, and right behind her came Freida.

As Freida entered the kitchen, Shlomo was just walking out with the lemonade. He accidentally bumped into Freida. Now Freida was covered in lemonade and soaked!

Mr. Yetzer Horah left his scooter parked by the side of the house and ran to the back door. Oh, he had the perfect idea! He was going to help these children fight with each other. He knew how easy it was for people to fight-even about silly things. Mr. Yetzer Horah also knew that Hashem likes when there is peace in the home and everyone is nice to each other. He was going to try to get these children to do the opposite of that!

"Freida," whispered Mr. Yetzer Horah, "look at you! You are soaked! It was so not nice of Shlomo to spill that lemonade on you. He probably did it on purpose! Now you'll have to change, and you might even smell like lemonade a whole day! Go yell at him! He did such a mean thing to you!"

Before thinking anything through, Freida opened her mouth. "SHLOMO!!" she yelled. "Why did you spill that lemonade all over me? You are really not nice! You meanie! I don't forgive you!"

Then Mr. Yetzer Horah quickly went over to Shlomo. "Shlomo, yell back at her! Do you hear how she's yelling at you and calling you a meanie?!"

Oh, no! Now Shlomo started yelling back!

"FREIDA! Why don't you look where you're going? Now Mommy has to make another pitcher of lemonade, and we'll have to clean up this big mess! I'm not a meanie-you are!"

Mr. Yetzer Horah clapped his hands with such excitement! Yay! He'd done it!

Middosman was out on his Middosboat. He was traveling to an emergency right near the beach. As soon as he heard on his radio what was going on with Freida and Shlomo, he called MiddosMalka.

Fluffy Brown answered the call. "MiddosMalka Control Center," she said. "Fluffy Brown speaking. How can I help you?"

"Fluffy Brown," said MiddosMan, "please let MiddosMalka know that there's a *shalom* emergency which I need her to take care of! I'm sending the details to her Middos watch. Tell her to please let me know if she's able to go and help out. Thank you so much! Over and out!" MiddosMan hung up, so he could get to the beach quickly.

MiddosMalka was baking cookies in the kitchen for an older neighbor next door who was not feeling so well. The batch of cookies had just come out of the oven when her Middos watch starting beeping. She shut off the oven and went to the call room. Fluffy Brown filled her in as to what was happening.

"Fluffy Brown," MiddosMalka said softly, "please call the Rainbow Fluffies. This is a serious *shalom* emergency. I will need their help today. Please let MiddosMan know that I will be there as fast as I can."

MiddosMalka looked at her Middos watch to see the location, and she set up the GPS.

MiddosMalka and the Rainbow Fluffies were at the end of the driveway in the MalkaMobile when the MalkaMobile stopped driving and shut off. Oh, no! The engine battery was broken!

"Fluffy Brown!" MiddosMalka called over her MalkaMobile radio. "Please ask Fluffy Black to come and bring the horses from the stables. The *shalom* emergency is actually pretty close by. We can have the horses pull us a few blocks. We'll fix the battery as soon as we get back. Thank you for all of your help today!"

When the horses were ready, MiddosMalka got back inside the MalkaMobile. The Rainbow Fluffies rode on the horses while directing them.

As they rode, the Fluffies and MiddosMalka sang:

MiddosMalka is coming your way!
With Hashem's help, I will save the day!

It wasn't long before they arrived at their destination. The Fluffies and MiddosMalka left the horses and the MalkaMobile near a tree and skipped down a long driveway to the house.

As they neared the end of the driveway, they could hear shouting. My, oh, my, was it loud!

Mr. Yetzer Horah looked up, and he saw MiddosMalka and the Fluffies coming! No, no, no, no!

As soon as the children noticed MiddosMalka and the Fluffies,
they stopped shouting.

"Hello, everyone!" the Fluffies called.

Baby Eli pointed to them from his highchair. "Fuffy! Fuffy! Hi,
Fuffy!" He waved.

The Fluffies waved back.

19

"What's going on?" MiddosMalka asked the children.

Shlomo and Freida told MiddosMalka what had happened and why they were fighting with each other.

"Aha! I understand the story," MiddosMalka said. "Let's talk about this."

Shlomo and Freida looked over at Mr. Yetzer Horah. They saw him listening in from the side of the yard.

Freida spoke first. "When I came inside and got soaked, Mr. Yetzer Horah gave me such a terrible idea. I was just so drenched from the lemonade that I wasn't really thinking. I said some mean things to Shlomo. Mr. Yetzer Horah loves when we fight." Freida looked at Shlomo. "I'm sorry, Shlomo. The lemonade spill is not such a big deal. I can dry off and change. And of course I forgive you."

Shlomo said, "I'm sorry I got you all wet, Freida. It really was an accident. I was walking quickly, and I just bumped into you before I could stop myself. I'm sorry I called you a meanie, too. That wasn't so nice either. I really don't like when we fight and yell at each other."

The Rainbow Fluffies looked at each other and said, "Hashem loves when there is *shalom* in the home. Hashem loves when there is *shalom* in the world! When there is peace and joy, everyone is happy too! We don't want to listen to Mr. Yetzer Horah and get into fights with each other. That just makes us all unhappy."

MiddosMalka nodded her head. "I'm sure you all like it when there is peace and your house is calm. You know, whenever someone annoys us, we can choose to not let it bother us. We can choose to forgive the person, for the sake of *shalom*. When Hashem sees His children happy with each other and doing their best to avoid fights, it makes Him so proud!"

MiddosMalka reached into her backpack and pulled out a heart keychain.

"Now children, this is a *shalom* keychain. You press the button in the middle, and it sings 'The *Shalom* Song.' You can keep it on your schoolbag, if you'd like. I have it in all colors, so you can choose your favorite. Let's listen to the song now."

26

MiddosMalka and the Fluffies sang and clapped along.

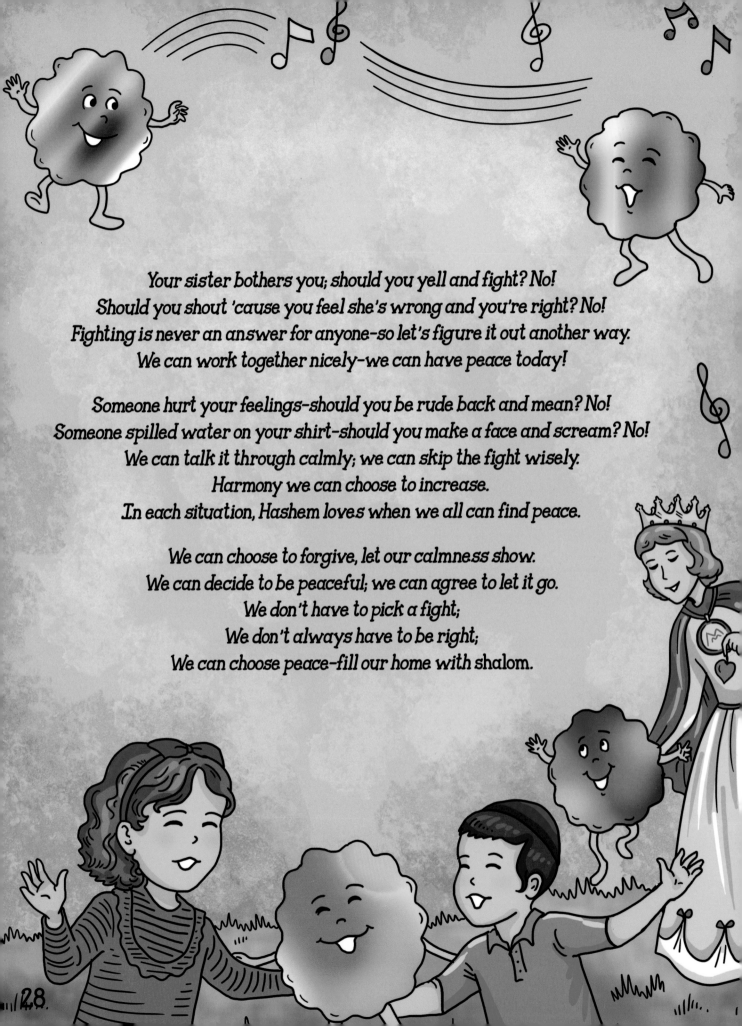

Your sister bothers you; should you yell and fight? No!
Should you shout 'cause you feel she's wrong and you're right? No!
Fighting is never an answer for anyone-so let's figure it out another way.
We can work together nicely-we can have peace today!

Someone hurt your feelings-should you be rude back and mean? No!
Someone spilled water on your shirt-should you make a face and scream? No!
We can talk it through calmly; we can skip the fight wisely.
Harmony we can choose to increase.
In each situation, Hashem loves when we all can find peace.

We can choose to forgive, let our calmness show.
We can decide to be peaceful; we can agree to let it go.
We don't have to pick a fight;
We don't always have to be right;
We can choose peace-fill our home with shalom.

Mr. Yetzer Horah was shrinking quickly. Soon he became so small, he couldn't ride his scooter anymore-he just didn't fit on it. He would have to leave it parked there until he had energy again. He started walking away slowly down the long driveway.

Everyone chose a *shalom* keychain for themselves.

"I'm going to try to be a kind sister and not fight with my siblings!" said Freida.

Shlomo added in, "It's really hard for me, but I am going to try extra hard to let things go and not get annoyed so easily. This way, we can have more *shalom* in our home. I bet Mommy and Abba would like that too. They definitely do not like when we fight and scream."

"That's the right attitude!" The Fluffies jumped
up and down. "We are so proud of you!"

31

As MiddosMalka and the Fluffies waved goodbye, the children's cousins began to arrive. It looked like it was going to be a fun and peaceful afternoon!

MiddosMalka decided to bring the cookies over to her neighbor as soon as she got back to her kitchen. She couldn't wait to do the mitzvah of *bikur cholim* and cheer up her neighbor!

As the Fluffies rode the horses back to the MiddosMalka Control Center, they sang:

Hip, hip, hooray! Hooray!
Hashem helped us save the day!
Mr. Yetzer Horah's overpowered;
He did not win today!